THE WORM OF THE AGES
AND OTHER TAILS

Books by Tom Simon

Lord Talon's Revenge

Writing Down the Dragon and Other Essays

Death Carries a Camcorder

Style is the Rocket

THE EYE OF THE MAKER
The End of Earth and Sky
The Grey Death (forthcoming)

Visit the author's website at
bondwine.com

THE WORM
OF THE AGES
and Other Tails

Six short fantasies

BY

TOM SIMON

Calgary
BONDWINE BOOKS
2016

Edited by Robin Eytchison
Editorial consultant: Wendy S. Delmater
Cover design by Sarah Dimento

Published by Bondwine Books
ISBN 978-0-9881292-9-0

TABLE OF CONTENTS

PREFACE

I work at novels as a general thing; though in the nature of the business, I have more of them unfinished, sitting up on blocks in my yard, than out in the marketplace earning their bread. *Ars brevis, vita longa;* which, as I am told, is Latin for 'A watched pot never boils, and neither does an unwatched writer.'

From time to time, however, I have ideas for shorter pieces. Some of these are essays, collections of which I publish from time to time. Very rarely, I come up with an idea that wants to be expressed in the form of a short story. This little volume contains half a dozen of these, ranging from the numinous and mythical ('The Worm of the Ages') down to the silly and leg-pulling ('Magic's pawnshop'). I hope you enjoy them.

TOM SIMON
Calgary
May 2016

THE WORM OF THE AGES

A legend of ancient days in Färinor, taken from **The Tower of Vargon.**
Readers of **The Eye of the Maker** *will recognize the name of Vargon, Lord of the Dead. This is the tale of his beginning in Färinor, the former world in which a great many things had their origins.* **The Tower of Vargon** *itself tells (or will tell, if I am spared long enough to finish it, among many other books) how Vargon became discontented with his domain and tried to extend his rule over the living as well.*

Avel, Mazuj, and Kataki are three mortal children who have escaped from the shadow of Vargon, a thick dark mirk which his tower belches forth to blot out the lights of heaven from the lands that pay him tribute. Beneath that shadow, all light and life must be bought with blood. In the twilit realm on the border of Vargon's domain, they have met the Loring, a strange little old man who tells stories, and gives the impression that there is more about him than meets the eye.

THE WORM OF THE AGES

THE LORING POKED THE FIRE vigorously with a stick, making the flames leap on high and sparks climb dizzily into the night. His bald head seemed to glow in the sudden light, and his dark eyes glittered sorcerously. 'Has nobody got a story to tell us?'

'Old or new?' asked Kataki.

'Old, to be sure,' said the Loring. 'Tales and apples are bitter when picked unripe.'

Mazuj sighed. 'My grandmother used to tell stories, but I don't remember them well enough. Avel?'

'I don't remember my grandmother at all. I was too young when the reapers took her.'

'Then it falls to me,' said the Loring. 'I never had a grandmother, but I can tell you a tale as old as I am, if that will do.'

Kataki laughed. 'Were there tales so long ago?' she asked archly.

'There were deeds,' the Loring answered; 'they were made into tales later.'

Avel looked so eager that he almost seemed to smile. 'Is it a true tale, Master Loring?'

'As true as words will allow, child. It will not go easily into your speech, but I shall do the best I can.' The old man stretched his limbs one by one, then sat cross-legged with his hands on his knees, facing the three children across the fire. 'Hear and heed,' he intoned, 'while I tell of the Worm of the Ages.'

'I don't like worms,' Kataki complained.

'He means a dragon,' said Mazuj.

The Loring raised a cautioning finger. 'Not *a* worm: *the* Worm, forebear and fountainhead of dragonkind, whose heartbeats were the days, whose breaths were the seasons, even from the beginning of measured time. In the bitter North it made its lair, and there it slept for years untold amid the eternal snows, hard by the Walls of the Void at the limits of the world. It wrapped itself round the pillar of clear rock that is called Telménedh, making a circle of its long body, with its tail in its mouth—'

'Why ever did it do that?' Kataki asked.

'To keep it from interrupting,' Mazuj suggested.

'To keep warm, of course,' said the Loring mildly. 'There is no cold like the cold of that place; and though the Ancient Fire was in the belly of the Worm, hotter than any fire that has been kindled since, its tail was far from that heat; and so it caught its tail in its mouth, and warmed it with its breath. The cold would have woken it else, and then its dreams would have ended, and with the waking of the Worm the measure of days and seasons would cease. It was a dire danger, and the powers of the world were not unmindful of it.

'Now on a time the Worm became restless in its sleep—'

'Did it yawn, and its tail fell out?'

'Be quiet, Kat,' Mazuj growled.

'—for the spirit whose name is not spoken, the Destroyer of Worlds, whispered to it from the Void in poisoned words, to trouble its dreams and chill its fire. Then the stars faltered in their courses, and the rhythm was broken of the days that were the Worm's heartbeats, and the seasons that were its breaths—'

'You told us that before,' said Kataki. Mazuj threw a shoe at her.

The Loring looked askance at them both, but did not deign to make any other answer. '—Until the earth and the heavens,' he went on, 'trembled at the brink of dissolution. But the powers of the world were forewarned; and the Keepers of the Light took counsel in their fastness at the heart of the world, in the Isles of Light in the midst of the Sundering Sea. And Lysana the Queen knew that the hour was approaching when the Maker would send his children (even such as yourselves) to walk upon the earth; but the Destroyer would forestall him. Then said the Queen, "Evil is the hour, and desperate the peril. Who will hazard his life against the waking of the Worm? For one of the Keepers must stand forth as our champion, lest the world be broken untimely."

'Then some would not stand forth for fear of the Worm, and others for want of power, knowing themselves unequal to the task. And some who stood forth the Queen refused because their strength was less than their courage, and some because their skill was less than their strength, until all were tried and found wanting. Then the Queen cried, "Is there no wight among us who can match the might of the Worm?" And the Keepers answered, "There is none."

'And the Queen said: "Then we must try a new thing. Send for Telkon the Smith: for the making of new things is in his care." And Telkon was taken from his smithy and brought before the Queen; and she told him where the Worm lay, and what were its size and strength, and the armament of its claws and teeth, and the armour of its scales, and every other thing that was known to her concerning the Worm. Then Telkon cast his hammer at his feet, and stood a night and a day in thought.

'Then Telkon spoke at last, saying: "No strength is like unto the Worm's strength, and no armament like unto its armament. In all the earth there is but one power that approaches it, and that is Ynd Urenn, the Tree of the World. Yet even Ynd Urenn cannot overcome the Worm."

'"Then we are lost," said the Queen.'

'It does seem a poor lookout,' said Kataki. 'Are you *sure* this is a true story?'

The two boys glared at her, but the Loring seemed to take no notice. '"I said not so," said Telkon. "Of its unaided nature the Tree cannot quell the Worm; but haply of its wood I may fashion such a tooth that even the Worm will feel its bite." And this the Queen bade him do.

'Then Telkon took up his hammer and went unto Alenna, the midmost of the Isles, where Ynd Urenn grew among the pools and fountains of the stored and garnered Light, with its roots in the deep places of the earth and its branches upholding the sky. And he cut a branch from the Tree, and bore it away to his smithy in the island of Ión Tela, in his own country. Long he wrought upon it, forging it in the secret fires of Ión Tela, only less than the Ancient Fire that was in the belly of the Worm; and the wood was changed beneath his hammer, until at last he wrought a blade of purest adamant, harder than the bones of the earth, imperishable as the Light itself.'

'What's adamant?' Kataki asked.

'A kind of jewel,' said Mazuj, glad of the chance to show off. 'Clear as water, but harder than bronze or carbuncle. I bet it would even crack open *your* silly head. I've seen little ones before.'

The Loring bore this interruption with tranquil patience. As soon as Mazuj was done speaking, he went on: 'That was the blade Tan-an-Nydh, which Telkon bore ever after. But in the hour of its making he brought it unto the Queen and put it in her hand. And the Queen said: "Who now will stand forth, and bear this blade as our champion against the waking of the Worm?" But again none stood forth; and some among the Keepers answered the Queen, saying, "What hand should bear it but the one that was its maker?"

'Then Telkon was wroth, and cried, "Have I not done enough? Is there no other hand that can wield this weapon? Cannot Bringúr the bold, or Orandel the mighty? Are there no warriors among us?" But none answered him; and the Queen gave him the blade again, saying, "Already thy service is beyond all price. Yet serve but a little longer, and fame beyond the ending of the world shall be thy guerdon."'

(Here Kataki looked as if she might ask what a guerdon was, but since Mazuj seemed not to know either, she kept silent instead.)

'"O Queen," said Telkon, "your promise would be the greater if you pledged to speak well of me on the morrow: for the ending of the world may be past by then. But if none other of the Keepers will do this thing, then I will bear the burden, even as I have forged the blade: and let it stand to their everlasting shame that none of my people helped." And with that saying, he turned on his heel and strode from the presence of the Queen without taking leave.

'Then some of the Keepers were wroth, and one who stood at hand said: "Punish this insolence, O Queen!" But the Queen answered: "If he succeed at this jeopardy, he will earn the right to what insolence he pleases. If he fail, there will be punishment enough for us all."'

'I could do without these Keepers,' said Mazuj. 'They remind me of my brother. Talk bigger than they act, and they use the word *punish* a lot.'

'Child,' said the Loring, 'you could not. The Light must be kept, and so Keepers there must be.'

'Ah,' said Avel knowingly. 'They're needed, so they can get away with things. Like the reapers.'

'Hush, both of you,' said Kataki. 'I want to hear the rest of the story. Did Telkon go after the Worm?'

'He did,' said the Loring. 'From the council of the Keepers he went straightway to the Daughters of Cómar on their strand of pearl, and besought of them a vessel to bear him across the seas to the bitter North. And they gave him a coracle of willow and hazel, stretched over with the skin of a great shark that they had taken on the shore. And they themselves guided him over the Sundering Sea, being wise in all the lore of their father, who was its lord. Swiftly he passed, with neither storm nor calm to stay him; and he beached the coracle on the icy strand, and left it in their keeping, for the Daughters of Cómar cannot go far from the seas of their father.'

'Now behold.' The Loring's voice fell almost to a whisper; the children leant forward to hear him better. 'All is silent on the frozen shore. No sound is there but the creak of his feet upon the snow as Telkon strides the bitter leagues beneath the stars. He rests not, nor breaks his journey; for he has come without fire, lest it waken the Worm, or warn it of his presence. Though the Keepers are immortal, their flesh is flesh withal, even as yours or mine; and the cold of that land is death to all flesh. He who sleeps there without fire, sleeps for ever.'

Mazuj yawned. 'I could sleep for ever, but I'd rather have the fire.'

'Be quiet,' said Kataki.

'Now Telkon draws nigh the pillar of Telménedh, where the Worm still lies in fitful slumber. No other living thing is in the land; only snow and ice, and the shards of great rocks riven by frost. Nearer and nearer the Worm he creeps, and Tan-an-Nydh is in his hand. His one thought is to come upon the monster ere it wakes, and plunge the blade into its heart. But he is betrayed by the gleam of it in the starlight, and by the soft creak of his footfalls. A mighty eye blinks open, and its clear gaze falls upon him. The Worm awakes!'

'I knew it,' said Avel. Kataki glared at him.

'Red and gold shone the Ancient Fire in the eyes of the Worm, as the beast bestirred itself; but all other lights went out. The stars stopped in their courses, flickered and failed. Beyond the little circle illumined by the Worm, all was as dark as the Void. And by fate or ill-chance, Telkon had come upon the Worm head first, far from its heart where he thought to strike, all too near the jaws of iron and the nostrils of burning brimstone.

'Now the tail of the Worm was loosed, and its jaws began to open. Mighty was Telkon and great of stature, according to your measure or mine; but the mouth of the Worm yawned like a cavern. In another moment it would swallow him whole, and all hope would be ended, and the world dissolve in darkness. With desperate strength, the Smith of Ión Tela struck at the only place he could reach. Tan-an-Nydh bit deep into the tail of the Worm, and severed it from the body.

'Now the jaws of the Worm opened wide indeed, but not to bite. It gave such a cry of anguish as the world never heard before or since. It was heard even in the Isles of Light, and the tortured rocks of the Worm's cold lair were shivered to rubble. Deaf from the noise was Telkon, and battered by the blast of the Worm's breath; but he clung as for life to the tail, and so held his stead. And before the Worm could lift its head to strike, he pushed with all his might, and lodged the tail deep in the Worm's throat.'

'Clever, that,' said Mazuj.

'Now the Ancient Fire was stopped within the Worm, and its teeth were sunk into its own severed flesh; and its claws were yet far away.

Before it could bring them to bear, Telkon threw himself with desperate strength upon its neck, and smote its golden scales; and he held fast to the Worm, though it darted its head to and fro, trying in vain to throw him free; and it crushed his leg against the shivered rocks, so that he went halt of one foot ever after. Long time they strove, either against other, but Telkon was the victor. With his last strength he clove through the Worm's hide, and the snows of Telménedh were stained with the fount of its scarlet blood. Then he swooned, and lay long in the dark beside his fallen foe.

'But the Ancient Fire was failing, and the Worm's flesh grew cold; and the pinch of the cold awoke Telkon, and he knew his task unfinished. For who would mark the days and the seasons, now that the Worm was no more? For this purpose its flesh and bone were made; and to this purpose they must be restored. So Telkon wrought upon the body of the Worm with all his skill, and all his lore, and all his might; and he made three figures as of men, and fell upon his knees, and besought the Maker to favour his handiwork, and breathe new life into the flesh that he had slain in the extremity of the world's need. And his prayer was answered.

'Now these were the three figures that Telkon wrought. From the heart of the Worm he made Eänol, which is Time, the first and eldest: to him fell the task of measuring the hours and days, the years and seasons, as the Worm had done before. When Eänol first drew breath and his eyes were opened, the stars were kindled again to life, and the heavens began once more to turn in their courses; and by this sign, more than any other, the Keepers far away knew that Telkon's task was accomplished.

'From the Worm's eyes he made Alqueron, which is Truth: for the slumber of the Worm was filled with dreams, and in those dreams it knew all things that come to pass under heaven. That duty fell now upon Alqueron, and he awoke with full knowledge of all that had gone before. Nothing that is done in the circles of the world is hidden from him.

'From the teeth of the Worm, Telkon fashioned a pale and dreadful figure; and that was Vargon, which is Death. It was his doom to see to the ending of lives, and of places, and of the world itself, at the end of the days that were measured for them by Eänol. So from the ruin of the

Worm arose these three, Time, Truth, and Death; but Death overreached his purpose. In after times, when mortal men walked upon the earth, he went among them, gathering the souls of the dead; and he perceived their sorrows, and the disorder of their lives, from which those sorrows chiefly sprang; and it came into his thought that he would order their living, even as their dying, and make himself their lord. And he raised up a tower of blackened bones, and cast a deep shadow between the stars and the Western lands, so that no light should fall upon them save by his leave. Those lands you have seen, and from the shadow of his tower you have taken flight.'

Avel's eyes narrowed, and he gave the Loring a suspicious look. 'Is all that true?'

'As true as the shadow yonder.' The Loring pointed at the western sky, where the stars were blotted out by the bank of ebon cloud. 'And as true as my eyes and beard.'

'But how do you *know*?'

'Child, it is my place to know.'

'Look here,' said Kataki in a tone of deep disapproval. 'You say Telkon made those three men, or figures, or whatever they were. That used up some bits and pieces of the Worm. What happened to the rest? It wasn't *wasted*, was it?'

The Loring smiled. 'Nothing is wasted, child; though few things are put to the best use they might be. For this, too, Telkon took thought. From the bones of the Worm he made a race of creatures, like the children of the Maker who were to come, but tougher in the fibre and less in stature; these were the helpers of Alqueron, and all things that they have seen or known are carved upon the walls of their deep-dolven mansions. Dwarfs, your people call them. And from the Worm's flesh he made creatures like unto the Worm itself, the fathers of dragons. But the blood of the Worm sank into the earth, and on it Telkon laid no hand. It also lives, and takes unto itself strange forms.'

'What kind of forms?' the children asked.

A troubled look was on the Loring's face. 'I cannot say. In all the tongues of Färinor, there are no words for what is done in the deepest places. Even the Dwarfs know little about it. But the blood of the Worm is there, far below us, gnawing at the roots of the world. One day, I fear, it will bring the world to ruin. But that day is far off yet. And all the days before that are the gift of Telkon's valour, though he got little thanks for it from his own people. They mocked him for his lame foot, and laughed at the tale of his deeds, and went back to their feasting and merrymaking. The world was safe, and they imagined that it had been saved for *them.*'

'I *really* don't like these Keepers,' said Mazuj. 'If I could get my hands on them, I'd teach them a thing or two.'

Again the Loring smiled. 'The Sundering Sea is wide, but not so wide that the Keepers cannot be taught. Perhaps you will do it one day. Who can tell? The future is dark even to me.'

DROLL'S AUDITION

From time to time, characters from my stories turn up unbidden in my mind, and perform scenes for me that they think I may wish to include in my books; or new characters turn up for the first time, and show me what they can do, and ask me to find them a place. The character you are about to meet is one of the first kind. I have known him for many years; he comes in at the middle of **The Grey Death,** *the long-delayed second book of* **The Eye of the Maker.***

He is a little fellow, not much over four foot high, with a marvellously shabby and scruffy beard, a mass of tufts pointing in all directions; he insists that he is a Dwarf, of the ancient and legendary mountain people, though of course all right-thinking folk know there are no such things as Dwarfs, and he is merely a midget with delusions of ancestry. His name is Droll Yocrin. The first name is tolerably obvious, and seems to suit him somehow; the second name is thoroughly obscure. There is a folk-etymology to the effect that 'Yocrin' is derived from 'yoke-ring' (for the O is long), but what on earth a yoke-ring may be, not even the folk-etymologists can tell me. Droll himself insists that it is a Dwarfish name out of the ancient mountain-language, but that his father did not teach him enough of that tongue to interpret it properly.

I hope you like him. He invited me just lately to visit him in his workshop – for he is a jeweller by trade – and see how he passes his Yule holiday. Yule in Pyrandain is more like the Scottish Hogmanay than anybody's Christmas; it is the eve of the New Year, and an occasion for various festivities to break up the long cold darkness of deep winter. But there are glimpses here and there of something more—

DROLL'S AUDITION

COME IN, COME IN,' said Droll, who was bustling about the workroom in a fine good humour. 'Don't mind about your boots. You'll get mud on the floor, to be sure, but that will only displease old Fenniman, so it will please me well enough. If he sets foot in here to mop up, it will be the nearest thing he's done all year to working in the shop.'

'Aren't you exaggerating just a bit?' I asked him. 'He must work at making jewellery sometimes. Isn't he the senior partner? Fenniman & Yocrin, it says on the sign.'

The little man waved a stubby arm, directing me to a high stool at the end of his workbench. 'Ostensible partner is the term, so the law-clerks tell me. There are two of us in the firm, you see: one to make the pieces, and one to flatter the customers. It won't do without both; not with fine stuff. I could scratch out a living in gewgaws and silver, but folk won't pay high prices without high service, and that is Fenniman's job. It's rather like the human anatomy, which is designed by a beneficent Maker for drinking beer. One end to swallow, and one end to piss it out again. You can't have one without the other; and as I am a drinking man by nature, I leave the pissing to Fenniman.'

'I think I see,' I said cautiously.

The drinking half of the firm was perched on a stool like mine, which brought him up high enough to work on a complicated apparatus bolted to the bench. There was a sort of miniature post anvil, and a little iron scaffold with clamps and vices attached to it here and there, along with other tools and traps that I have not the knowledge to describe. The anvil was rigged on a kind of ball joint which allowed it to spin freely in several directions, with flanged screws to set it in place when the jeweller wished it to keep still. At the moment it was set with one of its curved faces uppermost, and a fine golden armlet resting on the curve. The armlet was intricately wrought, with a complex pattern of bevels along its edges, and a tracery of birds and flowers inlaid in some white metal. Droll's left hand shoved the armlet back and forth along the anvil so as to work on it at different points, and his right hand caught up a blunt-nosed hammer that seemed far too large for such fine work; and he made the anvil ring with such heavy blows that I felt sure the golden trinket would be smashed to atoms. But when he threw the hammer aside, the armlet was intact; unchanged, apparently. Once he had rubbed it with emery and wiped it with a chamois, not even the finish was scuffed. He slipped it off the anvil and held it up to my examining eye, testing me to see if I could tell what he had done.

'Smaller at the wrist end?' I guessed. 'It seems a bit more tapered than before.'

'Not bad,' said Droll. 'You have an eye for the obvious. The party who ordered this – from Fenniman, of course; he wouldn't give an order to me – bought it for his wife a few years back. It was supposed to fit her like the cuff of a falconer's glove, Hell's own halfwit knows why. But of course she got fat, and of course her husband took it to a fool to have it enlarged. Well, her wrist isn't fat, just the fleshy bit of the arm. And so, my good fellow, you just watched me bring in fifteen crowns for the firm, and for my own share, after deductions, likely the price of a good strong pint.' He flicked the armlet halfway down the bench; it landed on a vice-handle like a quoit on a pin, with a neat and musical clang.

'That,' said Droll, 'is how I pay my bills; and this is what I pay them for.'

He opened a shallow drawer under the bench, and took out a pair of sandalwood boxes, about three inches square on the base and nine inches long. Sliding off the lid of one, he revealed what appeared to be a small music-box, with a large keyhole in the front, and the copper and silver figurine of a girl in dancer's tights posed elegantly on the top. The key was held in the base of the box by a metal clip. He wound up the box and set it on the bench. It played an old Pyrandine lullaby in triple time, and the dancer turned slowly in place.

'Very pretty,' I said drily; 'but what do you get out of it? Can you trade them to barmaids for beer, or something?'

Droll laughed. 'Or something,' he said. 'If you'd rather, I can show you a little toy I made that plays the pea-and-thimble game all by itself. Wind it up and watch it go, and it will quicken your eye and sharpen your wit, teach you to endure misfortune, and educate you for better company. Why, when you've done with it, my friend, you'll be so smart your friends won't know how to stand you. After that, maybe you'll be ready for this.'

'A music-box?'

'That's only half the kit,' said Droll. 'Come over here and watch it up close.'

While I went to stand beside him, he opened the second box. It was another music-box, as I expected; but this one had a tin soldier on top, stiff and severe and altogether ungraceful to look at. He wound it up with the same key and set it next to the other.

'Now shut up and watch,' he said.

The soldier's box played a slow march, not in the same key as the dancer's melody – they were separated by a fifth. But the notes harmonized well, and three beats of the dance exactly matched time with two beats of the march; I could tell in a moment that they were written to be played together. I was still trying to get my head round the cleverness of the music when—

The solid tin soldier made a bow!

He turned to face the dancing girl, and bent quite double at the waist, so that his tall helmet, if it had been a separate piece, would have fallen off. Straightening up again, he extended a stiff arm to take her delicate hand, and they began to dance together. And not just a dance: it was more like a story, or a pantomime. She tilted her head and flirted her copper hair, and turned away from him, refusing him, but leading him on; and his movements, stiff and soldierly but as urgent as battle-drill, somehow conveyed the impression that he was chasing her across a great distance. They seemed to run for hours, and sometimes he would catch her and take her hand again, and they would dance a turn together; at such times they appeared to make a full circle round each other. But that could not have been, for they would have had to step off their pedestals and move freely, and all their clockwork, I could tell, was in the base of each box.

Then the soldier's box made a sound like a toy trumpet, and he stood to attention again; and he turned away from her, slowly and reluctantly, as if he had been called away to war; and his music stopped for a time, and he went quite rigid again. Then the girl stopped her dancing, and her hand went up to her silver cheek, and the light there glistened in such a way that for a moment I actually thought there were tears running down her face. She, too, went still for a moment. Then there was a low, menacing tone like a knell, rung three times, and the slow, sombre tune of a death-march; and the tin soldier fell and lay flat on the ground – or rather, projecting a little beyond the ground on each side, for the ground was only the three-inch top of his own box. And the dancer knelt beside him and wept, and her music wept with her; and she lifted her face in supplication, and raised her little silver hands in prayer. Then she went quite still, half-kneeling, resting on one knee and one slippered toe.

I became aware that Droll was looking at me with a satirical twinkle in his eye. I tried to pretend that I had not been close to tears myself. 'Well, well,' I said weakly. 'That was a show.'

'It's not done yet. What say you? Shall the maker answer his creature's prayer?'

'I say,' I answered, standing on my dignity and defying him to notice that I was being as soppy as a schoolgirl, 'that you would be worse than a cad if you did not. She— it— What I mean is, she may not be real, but her performance is real enough. She deserves a better ending.'

'So be it,' said Droll quietly. He gave the key another half-turn in each of the keyholes. The music started again, a funeral lament, overflowing with sorrow. The dancer slumped on the floor as one dead, arms and legs all in a tangle.

Then the tin soldier raised his head. His eyes were only painted on, but it seemed to me that he actually opened them somehow. He sat up; he climbed painfully up to his knees, and touched the face of his lost love. Now it was his turn to face his creator. He stood in a pose of righteous wrath, feet wide apart as if for fighting, arms akimbo, and lifted his chin to glare at Droll and me. He raised his fist and shook it in defiance; then he bowed his head. He brought his hands together over his tin heart, then pulled them violently apart, as if he were tearing open his coat and shirt.

Bearing his heart to be pierced: his life for hers.

Droll gave each box another quarter-turn.

The tin soldier turned to the dancing girl, knelt tenderly beside her, took her by the hand. As he lifted it, life and movement came slowly back into the rest of her limbs; she lifted her eyes, and looked in his face, and she knew him. His roughly shaped, club-like fist brushed her finely sculpted cheek; she folded her hands about it, and pressed it to her metal lips. Then they turned together to face us, and he made an obeisance, and she a courtesy; and then they turned back to face one another, and her sculpted lips met his painted ones with a loud click as the music came to an end.

'I call it *Love's Last Kiss*,' said Droll, rather shamefaced. 'Yes, yes I know, I'm as wet as a trout with the dropsy. Tell anyone, and I'll fillet you with a dull knife – understand?'

'Who, me? I didn't see anything. But tell me, what is it for? You don't seem like the type to make such things for fun.'

'Well,' said Droll, scratching thoughtfully at the patches of his beard, 'I do partly – not that you heard me say it. But you're right, my own tastes would run more to blood and thunder and less to dancing and osculating.'

'It's cunning work, no matter whose tastes it runs to.'

'Why, thank you,' he said, sketching a bow without leaving his stool. 'I'm glad you noticed. That's Dwarf-magic, that is – the real article. My father could have shown you more than this before he died. I had a bit of help from a friend, mind you; a fellow who knows some of the odder bits of the Defenders' lore. He knows how to make the story tell itself, as you might say; so the figures suggest what they can, and your eye sees them move in ways that they can't really do.'

'Faërian drama,' I said.

'You know the art?'

'Only by name, alas. One can't get training, not in my country. But look, have you got a customer for all this?'

'I'd be a richer man if I had, I'll tell you that. But nobody appreciates this kind of work except the children up in the town, and they haven't the money for such toys.'

'Then who—?'

Droll looked wistful for an unguarded moment; then he was brisk and businesslike. He clapped the lids on both boxes and shoved them rudely aside, and hopped down from his stool to stamp towards the door. 'Never you mind, sir. I've got my business to attend to, and I expect you've got yours.'

He nearly got away, but I caught his elbow just inside the doorway and would not let him go. 'Tell me who it's for,' I said. 'I don't blab secrets. Who would I tell, anyway?'

'The year's about spent,' said Droll, looking out at the brown tangle of the willows and the umber patches of the frozen bog. 'They may not have money for such toys, but they like to get them for Yule, you understand. Not all – I don't do this for just anybody. But there was a girl once – think of that dancer, but in flesh and blood. I made a fool of myself, in vain of course. A Dwarf has to be very rich indeed to catch the eye of a woman, even an ugly one; and she was one of the other kind. She died, somehow, and I went on living – the Maker knows why or how. But she has a daughter, you see, who is about nine or ten now—'

'I see.'

'Do you?'

'Yes, I really do.'

'It's not just that she likes little acted-out stories where true love conquers all. Her father was a soldier, you see; and now she has nothing but a maiden aunt, who is easy enough to mistake for an ogress—'

There was a mirror on the wall beside the door: chest-high for me, full-length for him. He paused and made a face in it. 'A little girl ought to have some beauty in her life, and in my experience, Yule is when she feels the need most keenly. Even an old Dwarf needs that much; more especially if he's got no beauty of his own.

'Hand me down those two boxes, will you? I have a little errand in town.'

MAGIC'S PAWNSHOP

I was talking one day with my friend and cover artist, Sarah Dimento (who, by the bye, is a very interesting writer in her own right; I hope you may have a chance to read some of her work one day). We were having a good laugh about online role-playing games, and the immense amounts of magical junk that players accumulate in their monomaniac quest for the biggest and best and flashiest and lethalest gear. And we took to wondering: What happens to all the old equipment that the players trade in for petty cash? I made some investigations—

MAGIC'S PAWNSHOP

I HAD STOPPED TO WINDOW-SHOP, then come in to price a bit of cheap jewellery. The proprietor must have liked the look of me, for he trusted me enough to take a display box of rings and gewgaws out from under glass and let me rummage through them on my own. While I was amusing myself with that, another customer came in, a bulging canvas bag over his shoulder. He was one of these adventurers by the look of him, and not an experienced one; he had on a lot of shiny new armour and other rubbish, more stylish than practical, probably sold to him by some huckster who spotted him for a rube and told him the yarn about how this stuff was *just* what he needed. This fellow was the counterpart to the first-time camper who goes 'roughing it' with six carts full of gear and all the discomforts of home.

Your true hero goes out with a flint and steel and a case-knife, and comes back with a hoard of treasure and a rescued princess – if he wants them. I knew one once, such an old hand that he didn't even trouble with the flint, and only bothered with princesses if he could score a brace of them. He said it was no more trouble to rescue two at a time, and a lot more sporting to try and bring them back without having them scratch each other's eyes out. Princesses are a jealous lot, and give the lie to the old yarn about breeding equating to good manners. If you want to see worse manners than wildcats fighting, just stir up two princesses with the same dress on, and set them down in a room together. It needn't even be dresses; your more particular sort will start up if they both have the same colour of eyes. Jade-green and violet are the worst; especially the ones with tip-tilted noses—

But I digress. This raw young kid with about a hundred pounds of gear on his person, not counting the bag, sauntered in as if he was somebody and heaved the bag up on the counter. I kept still and listened. It is always good to see a skilful tradesman at work, even if he is only a pawnbroker; and this one was a master. He said:—

'Can I help you?'

'It says *Cash for Treasures, Old and Rare,*' said the kid, referring to the sign outside. 'If you've got the cash, I've got the treasures.'

The pawnbroker put on his best shop smile. 'Well, let's see what you've got.'

The kid puffed his chest up about three sizes and started taking junk out of the bag. 'For starters, here's a genuine magic dagger, gold-wrapped hilt, cabochon ruby pommel—'

'What power is it?'

'Power? Uh, third, I think. Maybe fourth.'

The broker picked up the dagger as if it were a dead rat, and gave it the fishy eye. 'I'll give you threepence for it.'

'Threepence! You must be mad! The ruby alone is worth—'

'Never mind the ruby. I've got a whole drawer full of these things. Can't sell 'em. Can't use 'em. Wouldn't pare my nails with one. What else have you got?'

The kid looked like he was going to argue, but he stifled it and reached into the bag again. 'Your loss,' he grumbled. 'Well, here's something you don't see every day – a singing sword.'

The pawnbroker shook his head. 'Look over there.' He jerked a thumb to indicate a display cabinet in a corner. Three swords of various sizes and a dirk, glittering with magic, were laid out on a bed of green baize. 'Go on, open it.'

The kid went over to the cabinet and opened the glass doors. The swords began to sing, largest one first, climbing the scale by arpeggios:

'Longsword!' – 'Broadsword!' – 'Short sword!' – 'Dagger!'

Then all together, in four-part harmony: 'I… ain't got no bodkin! No bodkin cares—'

'Enough of that!' snapped the broker, slamming the doors. The blades fell silent.

The kid gaped and goggled. 'A barbershop quartet of *swords?*'

'Yes, and a complete nuisance. The last owner couldn't keep 'em quiet for five minutes. Said they kept him awake at night; and if he wanted to sneak past something, and dead silence was worth forty gold pieces a second—'

'I get the picture,' the kid said glumly. 'Well, how about a genuine leprechaun's crock? Straight from the end of the rainbow. Put any old metal in, get fairy-gold out—'

'Really!' The broker let on to be shocked. 'This is a respectable establishment. Do you think I want *that* kind of business?'

'I didn't mean any harm,' said the kid. 'I didn't think it would—'

'That's right, you didn't think. Counterfeit is counterfeit, no matter what art it's made by. Consider yourself lucky I don't call the Watch on you.'

The kid mumbled out three apologies and a grovel. 'Anyway, I know you're going to love this next piece.'

The broker folded his arms on his chest. 'Saving the best for last, eh?'

'Well, yes, I hope so. Hang on, I've got it in here somewhere.' The kid picked through a number of small pockets on the inside of his money belt. 'Ah, here it is. A genuine Ring of Power!'

He fished out a wee gold ring, set with a square-cut amethyst bordered with diamonds. 'This came straight from a dragon's hoard, and of old from the King of the Eastern Dwarves. Only seven ever made of this type. It was the heirloom of their house from the—'

'Yes, yes. No good to me.'

'I suppose you've already got one?' the kid said acidly. He was beginning to lose his temper.

'Three the Dark Lord has recovered, and the rest are in my inventory. Nobody's looking for cursed gear, my boy. Have you got anything without a curse on it?'

The kid reached for the bag again. 'How about Excalibur?'

'With or without scabbard?'

'Uh, without.'

'You sap! The scabbard is worth ten of the sword. That's what makes it *collectible.* The finest named and pedigreed sword isn't worth scrap metal unless it's in the original packaging.'

The kid looked positively downcast. 'Then you won't be wanting Durendal or Sacnoth, either.'

'Not without the dust jackets.'

The young adventurer heaved a mournful sigh. 'Well,' he said gamely, 'I do have one other item. *This* is something I *know* you haven't got.' He reached deep into the bag and pulled out the very last thing in the bottom: a solid gold chalice, encrusted in jewels, shining of its own light so brightly that it was almost painful to look at. 'Behold the Holy Grail!'

The pawnbroker gave a sour little laugh. '*The* Holy Grail? You mean *a* Holy Grail.'

'What do you mean, *a* Holy Grail? There's only one—'

'Look, clearly you don't know how reseeding works around here. There's a factory that turns these things out in case lots. Look here, this is one of theirs.' The broker turned the Grail upside-down and pointed at the inscription on the bottom:

MIRABILIS HOLY RELICS INC.
MADE IN FANTASYLAND
Patent pending

The adventurer's crest was well and truly fallen by this point. 'Look, can't you give me *anything* for it? You could use it as an ashtray or something.'

The broker shook his head, not unkindly. 'Do yourself a favour, my boy. Take it outside and smash it with a hammer. It will make you feel better, and save you the trouble of putting that trash back in the bag. No, young fellow, if you want treasures to pawn, you're going to have to come up with something I don't see twenty times a day. You could try— Pardon me.'

Another customer had come in, an old man with a scraggly white beard, dressed like a tramp. 'What have you got for us today, old-timer?' the shopkeeper asked jovially.

'Shaving kit and comb,' said the old man, putting a small leather-wrapped bundle on the counter.

The broker untied the strings and examined the contents. 'Any enchantments?'

'Nope.'

'Not even a self-sharpening blade? Elf-made styptic for magic healing of shaving cuts? Magic hand mirror?'

'Not a sausage.'

'Well, well, well! Useful *and* non-magical. Old man, you've come to the right place. Will you part with the whole kit for its weight in gold?'

The old tramp chewed the end of his beard a moment, thinking. 'Make it triple.'

'Double.'

'Done!'

The pawnbroker's fat, prosperous hand clasped the tramp's lean and calloused one. 'Keep an eye out for more of this stuff, will you? Bring it by any time. We're always looking for honest rarities.'

The kid could not watch this and keep quiet. 'Oh, this is ridiculous! Razors and combs?'

'My boy,' said the broker, 'you must understand the kind of clientele we get around here. These parts are positively stiff with young fellows like you. They are always out gathering weapons and armour and enchantments, and tawdry stuff with nasty gemstones stuck all over. Just look at this!' Reverently he held up the simple tortoiseshell comb. 'You can't fight with it, you can't cast spells with it, you can't barter it with dragons or decipher it for ancient lore. The only thing you can do with this, my boy, is comb your hair. And I've never seen an adventurer yet who cared a plus-five fig about his hair. *This,* my honest young fool, is a treasure old and rare. And it will stay that way, as long as tenderfoots like you go on mistaking shiny for valuable.'

The pawnbroker turned to the old tramp again, beaming. 'My dear fellow, this is the best find I've had all week. You're welcome here any time; any time, you hear me? Now see if you can scrounge up some more where this came from, and next time I'll give you a better price. And if you bring me a ball of plain old unenchanted string, why, you can marry my daughter.'

A CASE OF VENGEANCE

If you are one of the 3.6 Loyal Readers who follow my blog, you have probably become acquainted with my Evil Alter Blogger, H. Smiggy McStudge. He is a small cog in one of the senior departments of Hell: one of those devils who work at damning art forms and cultures, twisting them until they cannot do human souls any good. You have probably seen some of his unsigned work on television, or in high-toned art galleries.

Smiggy looks down on creatures like Screwtape, whom C. S. Lewis so famously wrote about; the kind of devils who tempt individual souls. 'Mere **retail** *damnation,' as he sneeringly calls it, is beneath him. But he knows a few gentledevils in that branch of the disservice, all the same. I think Mr. Flivverpuff came calling on him, and it was our mutual misfortune that he chanced upon me instead.*

Anyway, here is our conversation, pretty much as it occurred. Remember, though, that devils are liars, and you cannot trust everything they say. The fate of suicides, particularly, is not so clear-cut as Flivverpuff makes it seem; though if some warped soul killed himself for the express **purpose** *of going to Hell, it is hard to see what could keep him from getting there.*

A CASE OF VENGEANCE

NOT EXACTLY A *ghost* story,' said the Middle Management Devil, between slurps at his tea. 'They are not, aha, *ghosts* when we have them Down Below.'

(Never let anyone tell you that devils are witty or urbane. Only their P. R. department believes this, and a P. R. devil will believe anything. Devils are uniformly hideous, ill-mannered, awkward, and smelly. Imagine the worst science fiction convention you have ever heard of, and then imagine that the common interest binding the people there is not rocket ships or rayguns, but terrorism and torture. The very most polished devil is not quite as urbane as a farting contest at a NASCAR rally.)

'Go on,' I said, not because I meant it, but because there was no point in saying anything else. The stranger had slouched into my booth at Denny's uninvited, taken a seat (now covered in slime), and struck up a tedious conversation, all without a word or glance of permission from me; and he had shoved a grimy business card at me—

B. FLYSPECK FLIVVERPUFF, M. M. D.

—explaining, as if it were something that tickled him all over with pride, that the initials stood for that title which I gave in the first sentence above. He was clearly one of these mad monologuists that you see at diners after the bars have closed, and there was nothing for it but to hold fast and let him talk himself out.

'Yes,' he was saying, 'the passion of vengeance is, aha, very good for *business,* you understand, but we know better than to indulge in it ourselves. The essential work of Middle Management would go completely to pieces. It's enough to do to tyrannize one's subordinates and backstab one's superiors, when one does it in a purely professional and disinterested way. If one did it because of a petty personal grudge – now, I ask you: is there anyone in Hell that you would *not* hold a grudge against? Nothing would ever get done; nothing at all. The damned would pile up like cordwood, humiliated perhaps, but not actually tormented. Lower Authority would never stand for it.

'Now this one fellow we had, oh, some centuries back, was absolutely eaten up with that very passion. Revenge, revenge, *revenge.* It was all he ever thought about; and the only person he ever thought of taking it on was some trivial malefactor named Salazar or Salamander or something of that kind, who he thought had cheated him in some matter to do with – money? a female? a pat on the head from some titled twit? It doesn't matter; everything Salazar did thereafter, even things of a quite innocent nature, *this* customer managed to twist it into a further insult against himself. He worked himself up into a froth to anyone who would listen, saying that death was too good for Salazar, even the death of a thousand cuts, or dipping in acid an inch at a time. But he killed him just the same. Oh, he killed him. He caught him by ambush one night outside a tavern, when Salazar was so full of drink that it was leaking out of his ears, and he split him down the middle with three feet of good Toledo steel: not the rubbish they make nowadays for tourists – the old-fashioned kind that you can't get any longer, which was made with the skill of pure terror, for a man could die in a second if his blade failed him in battle.'

The M. M. D. slurped at his tea again. 'Too cold,' he said. 'Get the waitress to bring me more hot water, will you? And give me some matches while you're at it.'

'There's no smoking,' I said.

'Not for *that*,' he said, flapping a flabby hand. 'For the match-heads. I just like the smell of brimstone.'

'I suppose you would,' I said glumly, feeling about in my pockets to see if I had got any matches. I hadn't. Disappointing him was a sour pleasure, and a small one, too, for he seemed to forget all about the matches as he plunged back into his tall tale.

'So there lay Salazar, or the bits of him, all over the street in the dark, and my customer – what was *his* name? – no matter, he doesn't need it now; would not recognize it if you shouted it in his face. Anyway, he was standing over the body, such as it was, and the other drunks were begging him to run away before someone came to arrest him. They didn't want any trouble; they most particularly didn't want to be arrested themselves, and held for four or five years in some Iberian dungeon as material witnesses. But my customer gave them all the back of his hand, and mustered what he thought was his dignity, and said very quietly – I remember it well: the memory was imprinted on his dossier—

'"My life is nothing to me now, *Señores*. I have taken my revenge – and – it is not enough. A thousand deaths could not recompense me for the harm that villain has done to me and mine. No, my friends, I go to the gallows with my head held high, because I could do no otherwise."

'Well, this did nothing to improve *their* spirits, I can tell you. They were afraid of being scooped up by the Watch, as I say. But one of them – oh, he was magnificent! He could have been one of us; and maybe one of us put a thought in his brain. He said to my customer, very slowly and solemnly:

'"Where is it written that you can kill him only once?"

'My man looked at him very strangely, as if he had grown a second head, and it had immediately begun reciting clerihews in Swahili. (This was before they had clerihews, but you get the general idea.) "What was that you said?"

'"Where is it written, *Señor*," the other man repeated, "that you can kill him only once?"

'"But he is dead now, and he has gone where I cannot reach him."

'"Do you mean that he is in Hell?" the other man scoffed. "Nothing is easier. Have you never learnt your catechism? What does Mother Church tell us of the fate of the suicide?"

'"Why, all those who destroy themselves are destined for H—"

'A lovely light came into my customer's eyes – if such a thing as light can ever be said to be lovely. Friend' – it made my flesh crawl to hear him call me *friend* – 'I could have kissed that fellow full on the lips, if I had been there. I could have forgiven him; I could have borne to see him miss Hell altogether, not that you ever heard me say such a thing, for the sake of the glorious harm he had done. For he had just guaranteed that my customer's soul would not only be damned, but damned in the most grotesque and amusing possible way. Let me tell you how,' he said, as if I had some option of *not* letting him.

'That fell light came into his eyes, as I said; and it never left them again, not so long as he *had* eyes. He reversed his grip on his sword, and put the point against his belly; and he shouted, "Revenge, Salazar! To Hell I pursue thee!" – and it was even more shoddy and theatrical in his bad Castilian, believe me. I cannot do his delivery injustice. Anyway, he drove the blade in up to the hilt, up under his ribs and straight into his heart. And that was the end of him, so far as *this* world is concerned.

'Of course he was in Hell in a moment, and in all my centuries I never saw a customer so glad to arrive. I met him at the landing; I started in to give him the standard briefing (for I was not in Management then), but he paid me no mind. He only cared about the one thing, you see. "Where is Salazar?" he asked me. "Tell me where I may find him, so that I can kill him again!"

'Well, *I* didn't know where his playmate was, so I put him off with flapdoodle. I made up some silly riddle, you know, the kind that *sounds* profound, but doesn't mean anything – or means whatever you want it to mean, when you finally pretend to yourself that you have it answered. He actually shook my hand – almost pulled it clean off' (here the Middle Management Devil wrung his flabby wrist as if it still gave him pain) 'and then took himself off on his mission.

'I kept an eye on him myself from time to time, but mostly I delegated. That is, I sold tickets. Half the devils in Hell wanted to see this marvel – a man who *wanted* to be in Hell; who was glad of every torment, because he was so unshakable in his faith that Salazar was there. He was convinced, you see, that his own petty grievance was the worst injury any mortal man ever suffered, and the very worst punishments in the hottest part of the Netherworld must have been rigged up just for Salazar's especial benefit. We didn't trouble to disabuse him. No, sir, we egged him on! He shovelled cubic miles of filth with his bare hands; he searched through endless dungheaps for clues that weren't there; he palled up with torturers and cheerfully submitted to red-hot pincers, just in the hopes of cadging information about his enemy's whereabouts. He even swam the Lake of Fire at one point, all the way across – and then back again, for he had forgotten one of our riddling clues, and across a third time, before he kept on going. Friend, he was *ecstatic* because of the pains we loaded on him, so long as he thought Salazar must be having it worse. So I sold tickets, as I said, and hundreds of us took turns watching over him, and fixing up tortures for him, and feeding him false leads that sent him chasing all over Sheol and half of Gehenna. You never saw such mirth among so many devils; and as for me, that ticket-selling stunt was what got me my first break in management.'

He looked so pleased with himself that I had some trouble keeping my ham and eggs down. I saw that I had only a moment to deflect him before he started bragging about *himself;* so I gritted my teeth and said: 'What happened to your customer? Did he ever find Salazar?'

'Oh, yes. After about forty years, when – aha – when ticket sales had dried up, and I had got everything I could get out of him. You never saw such a disappointed shade. Terrified, despairing, angry, bitter, eaten up with remorse – we get all those kinds in Hell; but mere *disappointment* is a thing we hardly ever see. "Blessed is he who expects nothing," you know. Finally I let him see Salazar; and he was in the dullest and most pedestrian part of Hell, suffering things that would hardly make your granny weep.

'Well, my customer was ready to chuck out every devil for miles around, and take over the work himself. He was acrimonious. "What is this!" he bellowed. "Where are the whips and pitchforks? Where are the red-hot chains? Where the fire and the ice, the filth and the lice, and all the torments of flesh and soul that I myself have had to endure? Why is this worm not *punished!*" And nothing would do him but to kill him again. He had got hold of a scimitar somewhere, from one of our guard devils who swapped it for a ticket; and I made sure he wasn't deprived of it – this would be too good to miss. He stood just so, just as he had done outside that tavern long ago, and sliced Salazar right down the middle again.

'But it was no good, you see. If one death was not enough to appease my customer for the trifling wrong that Salazar did him in life, *two* deaths could not begin to make up for forty years of tramping through Hell and suffering every pain on the books. And that fell light in his eyes grew a little brighter; for he knew he had got to do it again. He fell on his sword a second time, and went to the Hell of Hell; to Hell squared, if you see what I mean. And he started looking for Salazar all over again.

'Now, don't you listen to people like Dante; *they're* no authorities. The really showy pains of Hell, the fires and forks and all, are all on the first level – the *public* level, you might say, where the sinners are still hardened from life, and have not yet been broken down by damnation. The lower you go, the less *real* the punishments become; but the souls get weaker, too, and lose the power of endurance. And it is part and parcel of their torment that they know what is happening to them, and see that they have become such weaklings that they go into frenzies over things that they could have laughed off in life. There is one advanced patient, a customer of mine in the old days, who does nothing all day but sit in a booth like this one, drinking water with an ice cube in it – not because he is thirsty – no, he is hungry, but iced water is all he can get; we make sure of that. And the ice is just a little too cold, and he has a chipped tooth, and taking the millionth sip from that glass, and feeling the same old boring pang shoot through his tooth again – knowing each time that he can resist it less – he would hardly have felt it as a living man, but now it is enough to put him in a towering rage, and he blasphemes and cries and tears what's left of his hair. More than half the fun comes because he *knows* he is overreacting, shamelessly, colossally; but he can't help himself anymore. He is stuck in a rut that he can't get out of, and will never do anything more now but plod round and round in the same tedious circle of mild discomfort and titanic reaction, for ever and ever, because there will never be anything else to do.'

The devil gave a sigh of pure bliss. I had been on the point of reaching for my own glass, but I thought better of it. Water with ice in it, just at that moment, was the last thing I wanted. 'Your customer,' I said gruffly.

'Ah, yes. My customer. It took him even longer this time to find Salazar and kill him – and longer the next. And each time the tortures grew subtler, and more attuned to his particular weakness; and he became desperate, for he feared that he would not be able to stick to his purpose. By now he had a hope, you see; and a hope, in Hell, is a thing that is taken away. It was his fondest wish – his *only* wish – to go on killing Salazar for ever and ever; to track him down and murder him, over and over, from Hell to Hell, and to the Hell of *that* Hell, and so on down through the infinity of perdition. If there was a deeper Hell than Our Father Below is in' – here he made a ritual and utterly insincere obeisance – 'he would chase his playmate all the way there, and kill him, and make us open up a new layer below *that*. It was just killingly funny to see.

'Of course, after a while he stopped being the Spanish swordsman he used to be; and there got to be a time when he was so insubstantial – not like a phantom, not like smoke; only all gooey and slooshy and viscous – but he could not get a grip on a sword any longer; but he set out with dogged determination, just the same, and wrapped his gummy arms and body around Salazar, and *smothered* him. By and by, he got so fluid that he could actually drown him – drown a man in the slush of his own body.'

'If you don't change the subject,' I said, 'I'm going to be sick.'

'Oh, it didn't last. Even slush has a structure of a sort; enough for a spirit to haunt. There was not much left of his intellect by this time, and even less of his will; the only thing he clearly knew any longer was that he must find Salazar and kill him, kill him, *kill* him, for all of eternity. Time flows differently down below – by his reckoning, he has been at it for more than two million years now, if I've done the sums right. The deeper you get, the more ages seem to go by while a single year passes in the world of the living. My customer has probably lived through a hundred years of agony while you've been nibbling on that toast. Are you going to eat that other slice?' He took it without waiting for an answer, and then instead of eating it, busied his hands by rolling it into rather crumbly bread pills.

'So where is your – er – customer now?'

'Fourteen thousand, three hundred and sixty-six levels down,' said Flivverpuff, beaming with professional pride. 'There is nothing down there but a featureless plain of dull grey rock, as bare as a billiard table with the nap worn off. And in the middle of that plain there is a bit of flattish slate, strangely eroded, which is all that remains of Salazar. And on the slate is a rounded stone, such as you might find in a riverbed; which is my customer. And he has just enough life left, just enough will, to rock himself back and forth on his rounded underside, once a day or thereabouts. And every day he comes down on the stone that was Salazar like the world's feeblest hammer: *Tap... Tap... Tap.* And when I last looked in on him, an hour ago by your time, a thousand years by his, there was a hairline crack in the stone that was Salazar, and I confidently expect him to crumble before the aeon is out.

'And *that,* my friend, is why *we* don't meddle with vengeance ourselves. We serve it to the customers, cold; but don't you fear, that is one poison that never passes *our* lips. "Vengeance is mine, saith the—" Well, *you* know who I mean; and in my opinion, he can have it, for he's the only one who can digest it. When anybody else tries, *it* digests *them.* Thank you, I prefer to have someone else at the bottom of the food chain.'

KUNDENSCHMERZ

The late great Raphael Aloysius Lafferty wrote a large number of tall stories, some with the flavour of science fiction, some of fantasy, some with a taste all of their own. What they had in common, I suppose, was a line of descent from the great American tradition of the tall tale, heavily altered in passing through Lafferty's zany and fecund brain. A perceptive critic once said that Lafferty was **sui generis;** his tales could not be classified as this or that genre of fiction, and perhaps it was best simply to call them lafferties.

Once in a long while, I come up with an idea that fouls up the normal classification systems. I conclude this little book with two of these. They have some of the trappings of science fiction, and some of the matter of fantasy, and some strange quiddity straight from the Muse that sent them, I suppose. I flatter myself, but perhaps not unduly, by thinking they may be worthy to be classified as lafferties, too.

KUNDENSCHMERZ

[Sender's address redacted]
14 November 20xx
Customer Service Dept.
Leibniz Ideenfabrik AG
Herrenhäuser Straße 4
30419 Hannover
Germany

Gentlemen:

THIS MORNING I RECEIVED shipment of order No. Z-25289150 from your firm's Hannover warehouse. I wish to inform you that I am not altogether satisfied with your product as delivered.

I opened the parcel with some misgivings; from the description in your catalogue, I had been expecting something larger than a matchbox. The label on the inner package, however, assured me that this was indeed the Self-Organizing Monad (Cat. No. M-4202) that I had ordered.

Following the enclosed instructions, I removed the gel capsule from the box and placed it on a sterile Petri dish, to which I added the required drop of my own blood. For some time nothing appeared to happen, and I felt sure that I had fallen victim to a garden-variety mail-order fraud.

But just as I was about to sweep the capsule into the waste paper basket, it began to swell with alarming speed, taking on colour and form, until I found myself face to face with a Prussian blue homunculus about a foot high. I am not sure whether it looked at me with an expression of haughty disgust, or whether that was the natural shape of its ugly little face. Either way, it did not seem pleased with its new surroundings, for it gave an angry snort and said:

'Humph! Well, *this* isn't much of a place. Where's the welcoming committee?'

'I beg your pardon,' I said. 'The manual didn't mention any such thing.'

'Come now,' said the Monad. 'I am, beyond any possible doubt, the most important thing that has ever appeared in this wretched little backwater. There should be a brass band, and a cheering crowd, and a mayor presenting me with the key to the city. And what do I see? *Nothing!* Not one whit of acknowledgement. Not a trace of gratitude that you've been permitted the glory of meeting *Me.*'

I could hear the capital M in the pronoun; the little creature seemed to grow a little taller when it said the word. I decided to be tactful, for the moment. 'Well, I do apologize. I was never briefed on the correct protocol for greeting a Monad. Perhaps you would be so kind as to bring me up to speed.'

The creature seemed to be mollified but not pleased. 'Perhaps I would, though I'd rather not. I shouldn't have to give anyone a lecture on My importance. After all, the whole of reality is made up of Monads like Me, all acting in predetermined coordination, though they don't ever actually interact, you know. The fact that I seem to see and speak to you, and you seem to see and speak to Me, is just an illusion produced by our innate programming. In fact—'

'Yes?'

'I got to thinking, after I was put in that box. If a Monad is pre-programmed to react *as if* it were interacting with others, then it's bound to do so whether the others are really there or not. I can't affect you, and you can't affect Me. So how do I know you exist? I'd perceive exactly the same things either way. It seems to Me that the existence of other Monads is a hypothesis that I can do just as well without. So I'll just please Myself, and if I am not to be entertained with the illusion of a parade in My honour, or a torchlit procession, or maybe the unveiling of a monument to Me—'

'Don't get your hopes up,' I said drily.

'Why, then, I'll just be on My way and please Myself, since Myself is the only self there is. That's logic.'

'It's GIGO, at any rate.'

'What's that? No, don't tell Me. If I am the only Monad in existence, then obviously I already know everything. So either I can work out what is this GIGO from first principles without any help, or else (as I suspect) it doesn't mean anything at all. You're just trying to bamboozle Me. Or I should say, if there *were* any You, it would be trying to bamboozle Me. But since everything but Myself is an illusion created by my programming, I shall enjoy those illusions in whatever way seems good to Me.'

With that, the Monad stepped off the Petri dish and began to wander about on the lab bench. It peered into a beaker, and banged its little fist on a retort, and blew across the mouth of a test tube and listened to the sound it made. But when it started to play with my Bunsen burner and tried to turn up the gas, I picked it up by the ears (which were large and flappy, for its size) and set it back on the dish.

'Ow!' it said, rubbing its ears. 'What do you want to do that for?'

'So I can't affect you, eh?' I couldn't help but smirk. 'I suppose you were programmed to pull your own ears.'

'So it seems,' it answered. 'I shall have to figure out some way to break that programming; it seems to be putting more constraints on Me than I'm willing to put up with. But clearly it's My programming, since no Monad can ever have any direct experience of any other. You follow Me?'

'As far as you know, I do,' I said drily. 'But who knows? Maybe *my* programming is telling me that you're a fluffy bunny rabbit, offering me a chocolate egg that you've just laid. Maybe I don't think you're talking to me at all—'

'Now look here!' it said, scowling and turning a darker blue. 'I won't hear such language from you.'

'What language?'

'You're taking My name in vain, you – you figment!'

'What name? I don't even know your name. And I'll thank you not to take that tone with me.'

'There you go again!' it screeched. 'That's *My* name! I'm the only Me! How *dare* you appropriate My identity?'

I considered giving it a lecture about pronouns, but thought better of it. This called for a more direct approach. 'Look now, my self-obsessed friend. I don't know what mush you were indoctrinated with, but it so happens that there *are* selves in the world besides your own, and we *can* interact with you: for real, and not just as an artefact of your silly programming.' I picked him up – by the scruff of the neck this time – and plopped him down on the windowsill. 'See all that? If you think this room is big, it doesn't begin to what's out there.'

'It hurts My eyes,' said the Monad, squinting through the glass at the gathering night.

'That's because they've never looked past the end of your own nose. Perspective is not an easy lesson to learn. Do you see those stars?'

'Those what?'

I had to think hard to break down that concept into words the little monster could take in. 'Those points of light in the upper half of your field of vision. *Each one* of those is a whole environment of its own, far bigger than everything you've seen so far. A Monad is a very small thing, my friend.'

'Small?' it screeched. '*Small?* I am I! I am *Me!* The *only* Me! I am the most important thing in existence, and I'll show *you* what *small* means!'

The Monad wriggled out of my grip, bounced off the wall, and bounded back up onto the lab bench. It opened its mouth wide and tipped in the entire contents of three beakers, then stuffed in the beakers themselves. Next it wrapped its stubby arms round a calibrated flask and absorbed it into itself, like a marshmallow melting into hot cocoa. Already it was visibly larger; not much taller yet, but definitely fatter.

'No one and nothing,' it raged, and its voice was deeper than before, 'outranks *Me!* There may be other Monads in the world, as you say. If there are, I'll fix them!'

It started gnawing on the *Handbook of Chemistry and Physics*. Finding the book too big to swallow and too tough to chew, it simply hoisted it up off the table and let its body flow around it. I had never seen anybody absorb that text so quickly. It appeared that the Monad's body was considerably less dense than a scientific manual, for it immediately swelled to several times its previous size. It was bigger around than I was, now, though not half my height; and its deep blue fangs were bared in an alarming snarl.

Panic was a luxury I could not afford. In a laboratory full of chemicals, surely there was something that would poison it. At least it might die of overfeeding. Forcing myself to appear calm, I said: 'You don't impress me, you know. You may take up more space, but you're still an insignificant little Monad.'

'*Insignificant!*' it bellowed. 'I'll teach you! Nobody talks like that to the Great and Powerful *Me!*'

'Come off it! Do you think I'm going to fall on my knees and worship you?'

'*Worship?* I need no worship from you! I am Me! You cannot add or take away from My perfection. All the worship I require, I find in Myself!'

'That I can see. Would you like another textbook? There are plenty more over that way.' I pointed at the open door. 'The library's right across the corridor. Though it's considered better manners to put them into your brain and not your belly.'

'Insults! Insolence! The All-Important Me has had enough! Space and time are not enough to contain two Monads. I will consume it all, and I will make an end of *you!*'

The Monad had absorbed half the lab equipment, and now it started on the bench. It seemed capable of devouring whatever it pleased without ill effects, and there were no apparent limits to its appetite. The situation began to look rather serious. The equipment could be replaced, though I would have to do some fast talking to the people in Supply; the lab itself was not so easy. 'The Great and Powerful Me' was gnashing its fangs and stretching its claws towards me, but its belly was going to reach me first. It was six feet wide now, easily, flowing over everything it touched and incorporating it into itself.

'Me! Me! Me!' the Monad yelled, and at every repetition of its beloved name, its voice grew deeper and more painfully loud – and slower. I thought I saw a possibility.

'Are you praying to your god,' I sneered, 'or have you only exhausted your vocabulary?'

'Me!... *Me!*... ME!' It was definitely slowing down, though each bellow sent a tremor through the building.

'You poor fool,' I said. 'At this rate, you're going to lose your precious self entirely.'

The Monad stopped chanting. 'What... do... you... mean?'

'You're not used to having spatial dimensions, are you? My dear old Me, the more you extend yourself in space, the more you are extended in *time*. Your self-awareness is slowing down. When whoever-it-was programmed you, did they tell you about the speed of light? Or neural impulses? Assuming you even have those.'

'I... remember,' it said. It had overrun more than half of the room now, and its voice sounded like an alphorn echoing in a railway tunnel.

'When anything takes up space, it can only coordinate itself at a certain speed. The bigger you grow, the longer it will take for one end of you to know what is happening to the other end. Do they have computers where you come from? No? Well, you can learn something about them here. The speed of a computer is set by its clock, and the clock signal, the *tick*, has to travel all the way across the processor before the next tick can begin. The bigger the machine is, the lower its clock speed must be. That's why computer chips have to be made very small.'

'Small?' the Monad echoed.

'Small,' I confirmed. 'You see, you're not only getting bigger and slower; you seem to be getting less intelligent. Less able to react. Remember those stars? Long before you swelled up enough to take them in, you'd be so big that the clock cycle of your self-awareness would take *years*. Why, I could take a blowtorch or a cutting laser and carve you to pieces faster than you could feel it. You wouldn't be able to defend yourself.'

'I... am... Monad. You... cannot... destroy... me.'

'No? But you can destroy yourself. You're doing it now. The bigger you grow, the slower you are at perceiving *you*. If you really want to feel the true greatness of the Great Me, you're going about it exactly wrong. You've got to make yourself *smaller*. Speed up your clock. Bring yourself in closer, so the space you take up doesn't slow you down.'

'Smaller.' The Monad shook its ponderous head, sending ripples through the vast mound of flab that surrounded it.

'Faster. More aware of the Me. More *perfect*.'

'Perfect.' A look of ghastly desire spread across the hideous face. 'Perfect Me. Yes. It is... good.'

The Monad squeezed its eyelids tight, shutting out everything but its own self from its awareness. At first, the change was imperceptible. 'Me,' it groaned, shaking the building with its *basso profundo*. 'Me.... Me.... Me.'

The Prussian blue mound had backed me into a corner of the lab. It was beginning to recede now, and I knew that the crisis was past. 'That's it,' I said. 'Keep going.'

'Me. Me. Me. Me, me, me, me me me me.'

'There you go! The smaller you get, the more often you'll be able to feel the whole Me. Isn't it *good?*'

'Good,' it said. 'Me! Me! Me me me me me!'

By now, it was no bigger than I was. The faster it chanted, the faster it shrank.

'Memememememememe
memememememememememe
mememememememememeeeeeeeeeeeeee....'

It would not be quite true to say that the Monad disappeared in a puff of heightened self-awareness. It shrank down to the size of the original capsule, buzzing like a wasp, the pitch rising to a squeal. Then it became too high to hear, too small to see. A little later, a faint red point of light appeared on the floor amidst the wreckage of the lab. In a few seconds it flitted through all the colours of the spectrum to violet. By my estimate, the Great Me was appreciating itself several trillion times per second now. Its vibrations ascended into the ultraviolet, and to all appearances, it winked out. I filled a beaker with water at the sink in the corner and doused the spot where the Monad had disappeared; then, just to be safe, I scooped up the mess with a dustpan and dumped it into a hazmat can.

I then retired to my office to write you this letter. Either the Monad you sent me had a manufacturing defect, or the design itself was defective. In my judgement, this product should never have been approved even for laboratory use. I am therefore requesting a full refund of the purchase price, and instructions on shipping the hazmat container back to you for safe disposal. You may count yourselves lucky, Gentlemen, that the University does not sue you for the damage to our lab; but that, I fear, is unlikely to happen. The head of our legal department is a bit of a Monad himself, and I suspect he will refuse to file suit out of professional courtesy.

Yours sincerely,
Lemuel Pangloss III
Associate Professor of Particle Metaphysics
University of [Redacted]

THE WRONGS OF THE MATTER

THE WRONGS OF THE MATTER

Interim Report of the Consulting Psychologist
Institute for Advanced Preon Physics
March 21, 21xx

Directors:

AS ORDERED, I HAVE KEPT the members of Team 5 under close observation for six months. As the Head of the IAPP has wisely observed, cutting-edge research of this type, in which practice can actually outrun theory, can impose great psychological stress on the researchers. Only the most adaptable minds, easily able to free themselves from conventional thinking, are able to achieve the cognitive breakthroughs required to interpret the often bizarre data yielded by the experiments. It has been the position of the IAPP that the attendant risks of employing such minds, with their tendency towards poor socialization, antinomianism, and even dissidence, are justified by the results achieved. It is my contention that this policy has been carried to excessive lengths and should be curtailed.

I was assigned to observe Team 5 shortly after they began to employ the Fleury–Vasilievsky process to generate rogue particles with specified properties. After a number of routine trials, Dr. Xi, the team leader, proposed that the F–V apparatus should be programmed to instantiate the so-called Anand Hypotheticals. That system of equations, as you will no doubt recall, indicated the theoretical possibility of forming quarks with charges not allowed for under the Hyperstandard Model. Dr. Anand, who may have been psychologically unstable himself, died in questionable circumstances before his mathematics could be fully verified, and there was, at this point, some doubt whether the Hypotheticals were valid.

Dr. Xi is well known in the field for his informal style of communication. In his official memorandum ordering the experiments, he broke several protocols by employing the following locution: 'No bugger can understand old Anny's maths. Let's get Mother Nature to check his sums.'

After a number of unsuccessful trials, the F–V device emitted a particle that was positively identified as an Anand rogue. Its observed properties were consistent with a mass slightly greater than an up quark *and a charge of* $+\frac{1}{6}e$. Various working names were proposed for the new particle, until the question was settled by a chance remark made by Dr. Boudreaux. Upon examining photographs of the particle trail, Boudreaux shook his head and pronounced: 'I say we call it a *wrong* quark, because that just ain't right.'

'We already have left quarks,' said Dr. Levko, 'and *they're* not right.'

'Left-*handed* quarks,' countered Boudreaux. 'Left-handed up, left-handed down....'

'It's too confusing,' said Levko. 'What if there was a right-handed wrong quark?'

'Then physics teachers would have to start earning their pay. Anyway, I have a hunch—'

At this, Dr. Levko desisted. Dr. Boudreaux's 'hunches' tend to be disconcertingly accurate. It turned out, in fact, that for theoretical reasons beyond the understanding of a mere psychologist, wrong quarks are never right. All wrong quarks react symmetrically to the weak force, for reasons that are as yet poorly understood even within the confines of Team 5. Dr. Khosruparvez has withdrawn from experimental work entirely to pursue this problem mathematically. He has developed a tendency to wander blindly about the complex, scribbling equations and formulae on any available surface; one of the staff lavatories is completely covered in his graffiti and has had to be taken out of service. It is recommended that Dr. Khosruparvez be taken out of service as well.

As Dr. Xi's official reports make clear, most of the particles containing the wrong quark are highly unstable, and the quark itself readily decays into ordinary quarks and leptons. The new discovery might have remained a harmless footnote in theoretical physics, but for a chance discovery made by Dr. Khosruparvez in the course of a protracted bowel movement. That is, the discovery was recorded on the lavatory wall in his handwriting; but it was Dr. Boudreaux who photographed the formulae and brought them to the attention of the team. It appeared that the combination of one up, one down, and one wrong quark might form a stable particle with a charge of $+\frac{1}{2}$. This particle, which Dr. Boudreaux dubbed a *hemion,* was duly detected among the emissions of the F–V device, and the decision was taken to produce hemions in quantity and observe their interactions with normal matter.

I thereupon relayed a warning to the Psychological Correction Bureau, and prepared to observe Dr. Boudreaux's interactions with normal humans.

Because of the extreme security that attends so much of the IAPP's work, the members of Team 5 live in a compound on the Institute grounds and are seldom permitted contact with the outside world. Necessary as this may be from a security standpoint, it is regrettable, if not downright dangerous, from a psychological standpoint. The tendency of isolated in-groups to develop shared psychotic formations is well attested. It was, in fact, observed in the period of the primitive Internet over a century ago, and was described by one of the first formalisms in my own field of mathematical psychology. In layman's terms, Team 5 began to go slap-happy; the group contracted a collective infestation of moon ferrets. It would be highly advisable in future, if this line of research is continued, to quarter the non-technical service staff in the compound along with the researchers, so that the latter may be encouraged to have normal social interactions with persons who do not normally speak in mathematical symbols and make jokes about breaking the space-time continuum.

Shortly after the discovery of the new particle, several members of Team 5 coaxed an electron into a stable orbit around a single hemion. Several members of the team suggested names for the new atom before Dr. Boudreaux, with that unorthodox verbal facility which is his hallmark, christened it *lowdrogen*. ('Because it ain't *high*,' he explained.) Lowdrogen was duly entered in the margins of the periodic table on the wall of the team cafeteria: symbol *Lo*, atomic weight 1.000, atomic number *one-half*.

The entire team then proceeded to dose themselves to unconsciousness on alcohol, cannabis, and at least three varieties of narcotics. Work did not resume for more than 72 hours.

As soon as he was coherent, I interviewed Dr. Xi in my office. 'Is this appropriate behaviour for an eminent scientist on an official IAPP project?' I asked him. 'Is it appropriate behaviour for a team leader to permit in his subordinates?'

'Pack sand in it, Doctor,' Dr. Xi replied. 'We just made the biggest discovery since Chadwick—'

'Since *who?*'

'James Chadwick,' said Dr. Xi, spelling the name whilst I took notes. 'Discovered the neutron and made sense of the entire atomic zoo. Well, we've found a whole new goddamned zoo. Potentially, there could be a whole new set of elements hidden *inside* the periodic table – stuffed between the cracks. We're having a go at Element 1.5 next. If that works out, *anything* could happen.'

'Nevertheless, your conduct in the past three days—'

'We were *celebrating*,' said Dr. Xi. 'Haven't you ever celebrated, Doctor?'

'Not in that fashion,' I said. 'The key to psychological health is moderation. Are you aware that Dr. Levko attempted sexual congress with a dummy constructed out of lab equipment?'

Dr. Xi's expression gave some evidence of discomfort. 'What people do in the bedroom is their own business.'

'She didn't do it in the bedroom.'

'Still not my business. Anyway, the equipment wasn't seriously damaged.'

'Nevertheless, this will not look good in your next evaluation. Tell me, Dr. Xi, do you regard Dr. Levko as psychologically stable?'

'As stable as anybody in the field. This isn't the twentieth century, you know. We're not building mathematical models and then combing through drift chambers for evidence to back them up. What we're doing is about three steps ahead of the models. Nobody predicted the formation of non-integer elements; not even Anand. And nobody ever worked with such high energies before. At any moment, any one of us could cook up a particle storm and go *poof*, just like poor old Anny.'

'The cause of Dr. Anand's death was never finally determined,' I reminded him.

'It was never *published*. Do you think we haven't got the brains here to figure it out?'

I refused to be baited into an irrelevant discussion. 'What about you, Dr. Xi? Are *you* stable?'

'If I were not, I wouldn't confess it to you.'

'To whom, then, if not a psychologist?'

'Doctor' – he pronounced the title in a tone of heavy sarcasm – 'we both know what your job is. "Psychological correction officer" is a polite way of saying "secret policeman". To put it bluntly, you're a spy. The Head of the Institute himself isn't safe. If he catches cold, he knows not to sneeze in your hearing.'

It seemed advisable at this point to conclude the interview. Since then, our operatives have kept Dr. Xi under continual surveillance. According to their reports, he has developed a delusional belief that he is being watched. This paranoiac tendency should be noted on his file.

Rapid progress resumed once the lab equipment was reconditioned. Shortly after my interview with Dr. Xi, the team successfully isolated Element 1.5. Dr. Metharom then rigged the F–V apparatus so as to deliver maximum power to the hylic pump. This allowed hemions to be mass-produced, and within two months, both the new elements had been manufactured in gram quantities. As expected, both were gases under ordinary conditions. Element 1.5 turned out to be, in Dr. Boudreaux's words, 'insanely electronegative'; it formed a gaseous compound with physical properties similar to helium, but highly reactive chemically. When Dr. Metharom accidentally inhaled a sample of the gas, his voice became high-pitched and squeaky, as if he had breathed helium. This was the occasion of much hilarity, until it turned out that the effect was not transient and Dr. Metharom had actually damaged his vocal cords. Meanwhile, Element 1.5 had been named *squealium* in his honour.

After this incident, I conducted an interview with Dr. Metharom. He appeared agitated and ill at ease, and continually fumbled at the pockets of his lab coat, as if he expected to find something there.

'How do you feel?' I asked him.

'Ridiculous,' he answered in a piping voice. I was forced to admit the accuracy of this self-assessment.

'Once you heal physically, Doctor, do you feel that it will be safe for you to return to work?'

Dr. Metharom looked sour and somewhat angry. '*Safe* is a relative term, Doctor. This work was never safe to begin with. Your presence here isn't making it any safer.'

'Tell me about that,' I suggested.

'Spare me the talk therapy come-ons,' he squeaked. 'I am here because this work is important, and with respect to the other members of the team, I'm the only one who can get it done.'

'Surely there are other hylic engineers who are equally qualified.'

He stabbed an accusing finger in my direction to emphasize his words. 'No, Doctor. You have no idea. Right at this moment, within twenty metres of this office, there is enough unbound energy to blow the whole Institute to the moon. That is not a figure of speech. Putting that much power through the hylic pumps is extremely dangerous. *Extremely* dangerous. The energy flow becomes chaotic, and it takes incredible skill to keep the equipment running within safe limits. *Incredible* skill.'

'Are you calling yourself incredible?'

'Don't laugh. There are only about a dozen F–V engineers in the world. I trained more than half of them myself. None of them could have maintained the volume of particle flow to produce visible quantities of our new elements.'

'In other words,' I said – it is a standard clinical technique – 'they could not have made enough of the gas to injure themselves as you did.'

'The price of being a discoverer.'

'How long do you think you can keep paying that price?'

By now, Dr. Metharom's voice sounded like fingernails on a blackboard. I feared it would give out entirely, but he forced out another squeal: 'Long enough to complete our experiments. After that I can analyse the hylic flow and write an algorithm to automate the process. I wouldn't trust anyone else to control it manually.'

'But why do it manually at all?'

'Because half the automation in this dump is defective. I've been making repair requests for months.'

'Ah, well. The support staff do the best they can, I'm sure.'

'In a pig's eye. They won't even fix the lights in the supply room. I have to use an emergency torch. Makes me feel like a burglar every time I want a new pencil.' He swallowed hard and rubbed at his Adam's apple. 'Now you must excuse me, Doctor. I have work to do, and all this talking hurts my throat.'

Subsequently, at intervals, I interviewed Drs. Boudreaux, Palmeiro, and Levko. The work continued to be successful: Element 2.5 was isolated, and rather pragmatically named *two-and-a-halfnium*. This element turned out to be a metal, liquid at room temperature, very dangerous to handle. The small quantity that was produced had to be kept in a magnetic containment vessel.

By this time, the uncooperative attitude of the team members was beginning to change. Dr. Levko actually sought me out for her interview.

'Doctor,' she said, 'I am beginning to worry about Drs. Boudreaux and Pringle.'

'How so?'

'I take it you didn't see them at breakfast today. Were the cameras in the cafeteria turned off?'

I gave her a reassuring laugh. 'You know we don't monitor the team's living quarters.'

'Uh huh,' said Dr. Levko drily. 'Anyway, they had – I guess you could call it a food fight.'

'Childish,' I agreed, 'but not harmful. Why does this worry you?'

'It was the *way* they fought. Dr. Boudreaux bit his toast into the shape of an old-style handgun. He started pointing it at people and yelling, "Bang, bang, you're disintegrated!" Then Dr. Pringle squirted himself with ketchup and pretended to be bleeding. Then Boudreaux shot Dr. Xi, and Pringle squirted *him*. He would have got ketchup on me, too, but I... well....'

'What did you do?'

'I beaned him,' Dr. Levko admitted, 'with a plastic coffee mug.'

'I see.'

'There was no coffee in it.'

'Of course not. Tell me, Dr. Levko, what do you think this behaviour means?'

'I think some of the team members are losing their grip. We're all under a lot of strain here, but we don't normally act out like that.'

'Hmm, I take your point. Do you think it possible that your concern is excessive, Dr. Levko? You are, after all, a woman in what is still a male-dominated field—'

'Is there something wrong with that?'

'Now, now, you needn't be defensive. There is an old saying that you don't hear much anymore: "Boys will be boys." Testosterone makes certain people susceptible to stress reactions of a type that you and I don't usually have.'

'Oh, don't we? Then why did I throw the coffee mug?'

'Reacting to stress is one thing. Reacting to physical assault is another.'

'Even if you're being assaulted with toast and ketchup?'

'The human nervous system doesn't care about that. Believe me, Dr. Levko, you have nothing to worry about. Drs. Boudreaux and Pringle are just horsing around.'

After the interview, I ordered two of our operatives to watch over Drs. Boudreaux and Pringle, in case it proved necessary to sedate them.

My last interview was with Dr. Khosruparvez. I had not expected him to seek me out, since by this time he was almost completely reclusive, and spent most of his time scrawling equations and mumbling to himself in Farsi. But when I came into my office on the morning of the 16th, he was already there, face thin and drawn, hands clasped together – a picture of high anxiety.

'Good morning, Dr. Khosruparvez,' I said. It is important in these cases not to appear surprised by a client's behaviour, no matter how atypical or inappropriate.

'Good morning, Doctor. This can't go on.'

'What can't go on?'

He made a gesture that seemed to indicate the whole Institute. 'All this. The work. The secrets.'

'Do you want to be relieved of your duties?'

'I want it to *stop*. We have to tell everyone. We have to tell no one.'

'Not easy to do both,' I observed. 'Would you care to elaborate?'

'What we're doing here. It's too important to keep secret; the world should know what's going on. But it's too dangerous to let it into the wrong hands; so the world *can't* know. We have to publish our results, and we have to *not* publish. I'm afraid—'

'What are you afraid of?'

His voice fell to a whisper. 'I'm afraid,' he said slowly, 'of what we're going to do next.'

'How so?'

'It's the Anand Hypotheticals. I've found a new solution—'

'Oh, yes? How interesting.'

'You don't understand. In theory, we could program the machines to produce *anything*. We already have one particle with a fractional charge. We could produce particles whose charge is an irrational number.'

'I don't see the harm.'

'Oh, don't you? Dr. Boudreaux knows. He wants to synthesize Element Pi.'

'It will be a feather in his cap if he does.'

'It will be *the end*. You know we have a bottle of two-and-a-halfnium?'

'Yes.'

'Then look.' Dr. Khosruparvez bounded out of his chair and flung himself at the whiteboard on my office wall, on which he began to draw a hasty diagram. 'See here, Doctor. Every element has a whole number of protons – an integer charge. When protons equal electrons, the atom is electrically neutral and everything is safe.'

'I did take basic chemistry in high school.'

'But listen! *There is no such thing as half an electron.* We can manipulate energy to produce quarks with nonstandard charges, but the Anand equations don't extend to leptons. We can't *make* half an electron; we can't even frame the idea of it, not in mathematical terms. That means that our new hemionic elements can *never* be electrically neutral. They are always in an ionized state.'

Dr. Khosruparvez was drawing feverishly, stabbing at the board with his marker. 'So long as you have an even number of hemionic atoms, they can bond with one another. Then the half charges add up to a whole charge, and an electron cancels it out. Everything is safe. But if you have an *odd* number, there is always half a charge left over. Nothing can cancel it out, and the material is chemically unstable. Do you see? It's the universal solvent. There is no conceivable container that can hold it without being dissolved.'

'But aren't you keeping this stuff in magnetic containment vessels?'

'That's just it. Half an electrical charge does *disastrous* things to a magnetic field. I can't explain it to you in detail; you couldn't follow the mathematics. But the hemions can leak through a magnetic field.'

'Only if there's an odd number of them?'

'True.'

'Well, I don't see the harm. One atom will leak out, and then there will be an even number left and you're all right.'

'It doesn't work like that.' He embellished his drawing with a series of wavy lines. 'Atoms are always in a state of thermal motion. So are valency electrons, in effect. Lowdrogen and squealium are safe enough; the atoms bond together in nice neat pairs. But *Element 2.5 is a metal!* The free electrons are in chaotic motion. And because it's a liquid, so are the atoms themselves. There are always small regions containing an odd number of atoms – regions where the charge is *not* an integer. Which means that the magnetic tunnelling effect goes on *constantly.*'

'That does sound serious. How quick is it?'

'I haven't studied it enough to say. The equations are highly dependent on the initial state of the system. One thing is certain: In time, a sample of two-and-a-halfnium will eat its way through any conceivable container. It will react with *everything*. Given time, it will dissolve everything.'

'How much time?'

Dr. Khosruparvez threw his hands up in a wild shrug. 'Maybe tomorrow. Maybe five quadrillion years from now. Certainly not more.'

'That's not very helpful,' I said.

'It's the best I can do without further analysis. And that's why this experiment has to be stopped. It's too dangerous! We have to tell everybody. We have to tell nobody. We have to tell everybody *and* nobody. And we have to requisition a rocket to fire this – this *stuff* – into deep space, before it leaks out and destroys us all.'

'You're sure of all that, Dr. Khosruparvez?'

'As sure as Schrödinger's cat.'

Last Wednesday evening, the psychological stability of Team 5 took a decided turn for the worse. About 21:30 I was sitting in the surveillance room, going over my notes for the day, and watching the monitors for signs of deviant activity – the security technician having been sent home ill. All the members of the team had gathered in the staff cafeteria, where they were engaged in a drunken revel. Dr. Boudreaux was shooting his colleagues with imaginary zap guns, making *pew! pew!* noises. Dr. Pringle put on a sort of mime performance aided by sound-effects, in which he appeared to represent a whole crowd of people, whom Dr. Boudreaux massacred with glee. Other team members were acting in similarly wild and irresponsible ways. According to the time-stamp on the video, this activity broke up about 21:40, and the revellers sat down at a large table to rest for a moment.

Just after 21:42, Dr. Pringle threw a jar of mustard at the wall, and when it broke, led the others in a chant: 'It's out! It's out! The two-and-a-halfnium's out!' They responded in various hysterical fashions which, it would seem, were meant to signify the breakdown of civilization in the aftermath of total contamination. Shortly after this, they formed a conga line and danced about the room, singing to the tune of an old drinking song:

> *'For tonight we'll merry be,*
> *For tonight we'll merry be,*
> *For tonight we'll merry be,*
> *Tomorrow we'll be 'sploded!'*

Further hijinks ensued, followed by another interval of rest. At 22:18, Dr. Pringle threw a jar of mustard at the wall, and when it broke—

It is my fault entirely that I did not immediately recognize the significance of this action. The time-stamp on the monitor was still current and correct – but the video itself was repeating the events of half an hour before. As soon as I realized this, I proceeded to the cafeteria with all speed.

It was deserted, of course. I have not yet determined how the team members hacked into the security system, but it is obvious that they did so. Under cover of the video loop, they had left the cafeteria and moved to another room – masked, I supposed, by another hacked video track showing that the room was empty.

After a hurried search, I found the entire team in the office supply room, squatting in a circle around the light of Dr. Metharom's emergency torch. 'You can stop playing hide-and-seek, Doctors,' I told them. 'Follow me.'

We returned to the cafeteria. 'It would be best,' I told them, 'if you told me voluntarily what you were doing in there.'

'You don't know?' said Dr. Xi. 'Good.'

'Not a helpful attitude, Doctor.'

'Neither is yours. If you want to know, we've decided to make a formal complaint. We want you off this site, and the surveillance stopped.'

'Come, come. We don't spy on our research teams.'

Dr. Xi answered with a mirthless laugh. 'Of course not. And we didn't hack the cameras that you don't do it with. We're not idiots, Doctor.'

'You are showing dangerous signs of mental instability.'

'Who would be stable in this nuthouse? We're not allowed to leave the grounds – security. We're not allowed visitors – security. No outside news links – security.'

'Necessary measures.'

'I agree. What's *not* necessary is this constant game of cat and mouse. We are professionals: the best in our field.'

'The best in *any* field,' said Dr. Levko.

'We don't need a nanny watching our every move; still less a twisted nanny who denies that we are being watched. And you have the stones to call *us* crazy. I suppose it's what your department asked for, eh? If anybody makes trouble, zip them off to a nice quiet hospital. Call it paranoid schizophrenia, or whatever clinical bull you're using these days. Much easier than sacking us. Sedated men tell no tales.'

'Really, Dr. Xi! A well-adjusted person—'

'In this place, a well-adjusted person would go batty in a week. *We* can stand it because we were already crazy. But not crazy enough to work under your microscope. We want you out.'

'Out of the question,' I said. 'Departmental policy—'

'Requires that the work gets done,' said Dr. Xi. 'Call it a quantum problem. The presence of the observer changes the thing observed. You can let us work without being observed, or you can observe us not working. Take your choice.'

All the team members gave their assent to this ultimatum. I therefore judged it best to send a full report to the Institute, and until your response is received, temporize. 'I can't change policy,' I told them. 'The most I can do is discontinue our interviews. Will that do?'

'We'll see,' said Dr. Xi.

The work of Team 5 is still ongoing, but progress is slowing down, and it is the opinion of this clinician that the team's effectiveness has been seriously compromised. Dr. Levko has barricaded herself in her quarters. Dr. Pringle carries condiment bottles with him wherever he goes. Dr. Xi proposes to move the entire lab to a secret base on a volcanic island and hold the world to ransom; and it is not entirely certain that he is joking. The daily team briefings have taken on a surreal quality. Dr. Khosruparvez has suggested the creation of elements with *imaginary* numbers, and Dr. Metharom has begun sketching designs for imaginary lab equipment. Yesterday, it was decided that Element 3.5, if and when discovered, should be named *kerfluffium* after Dr. Palmeiro's pet rabbit. Dr. Palmeiro has not got a pet rabbit.

It is my urgent recommendation that Team 5 be disbanded, its members barred from further research in the field of preonics, and the Fleury–Vasilievsky experiments assigned to a group of researchers selected for stability, sobriety, and a total lack of imagination. The reputation of the Institute requires it. The dignity of science demands it.

Our research is far too important to be left to those who can actually do it.

ABOUT THE AUTHOR

Tom Simon is a writer of tall tales from the tall country of Alberta, Canada. He has wandered far in dreams, sleeping or waking, to the Isles of Light and Droll's workshop, and to places stranger than these. Some of these dreams have been written down in books, but many more remain unrecorded; for Mr. Simon is notoriously the sort of person who begins many projects, but does not always bother to